Dear Parent:
Your child's love of reading starts here!

Every child learns to read in a different way and at his or her own speed. Some go back and forth between reading levels and read favorite books again and again. Others read through each level in order. You can help your young reader improve and become more confident by encouraging his or her own interests and abilities. From books your child reads with you to the first books he or she reads alone, there are I Can Read Books for every stage of reading:

SHARED READING
Basic language, word repetition, and whimsical illustrations, ideal for sharing with your emergent reader

BEGINNING READING
Short sentences, familiar words, and simple concepts for children eager to read on their own

READING WITH HELP
Engaging stories, longer sentences, and language play for developing readers

READING ALONE
Complex plots, challenging vocabulary, and high-interest topics for the independent reader

ADVANCED READING
Short paragraphs, chapters, and exciting themes for the perfect bridge to chapter books

I Can Read Books have introduced children to the joy of reading since 1957. Featuring award-winning authors and illustrators and a fabulous cast of beloved characters, I Can Read Books set the standard for beginning readers.

A lifetime of discovery begins with the magical words **"I Can Read!"**

Visit www.icanread.com for information on enriching your child's reading experience.

To Jill, who is the tseb—oops, I mean best sister
—J.O'C.

For A.O.'s best huggers, Madison and Connor
—R.P.G.

For my fav' Luddite.
Always looking ahead, over your shoulder
—T.E.

I Can Read Book® is an imprint of HarperCollins Publishers.

Fancy Nancy: It's Backward Day!

www.icanread.com

Library of Congress Control Number: 2015950808
ISBN 978-0-06-226982-9 (trade bdg.) — ISBN 978-0-06-226981-2 (pbk.)

16 17 18 19 20 LSCC 10 9 8 7 6 5 ❖ First Edition

by Jane O'Connor

cover illustration by Robin Preiss Glasser

interior illustrations by Ted Enik

HARPER

An Imprint of HarperCollins*Publishers*

Today all the kids walk
into school like this.

"Good-bye," we say to Ms. Glass.

"Good-bye," Ms. Glass says to us.

Then we all sit down.

Nobody faces Ms. Glass.

Why is everything topsy-turvy?
(That's fancy for
upside down and super silly.)
It's Backward Day!
Look what the kids are wearing.

Lionel has on sunglasses
and a tie.

Robert has on a tie and jacket.

Clara's hair is in a French braid.
Ooh la la!
It looks fancy and backward.

Bree and I have on purple hoodies.

We wear socks on our hands.

So does Ms. Glass.

She also wears a tutu for a hat.

I adore my topsy-turvy teacher.

First we all say the alphabet.

We have to start with *z, y, x*.

"This is easy," Lionel says.

He means that it's hard!

Next Ms. Glass reads us a story.

She starts on the last page!

“I don’t like Backward Day

at all,” Lionel says.

He means he likes it a lot.

Then we make name tags.
Here are our backward names.
They are nonsensical.
That is also fancy for super silly.

MY NAME IS
trebor

MY NAME IS
aralC
MY NAME IS
LENOIL
MY NAME IS
YCNAN

At lunch we eat dessert first.

Lionel has cookies.

Ooh la la!

They look delectable.

That is fancy for yummy.

“I won’t share with you,”
Lionel says.
“That’s not nice,” I say.

Then Lionel shouts,

“Ha-ha! I’m joking.

It’s Backward Day.

I’m saying that

I WILL share my cookies.”

He gives me two!

In the yard
we divide into teams
for races.

We have to run backward.

It is extremely hard.

Extremely is fancy for very.

“I’m sorry we’re
on the same team,”
Lionel says to me.

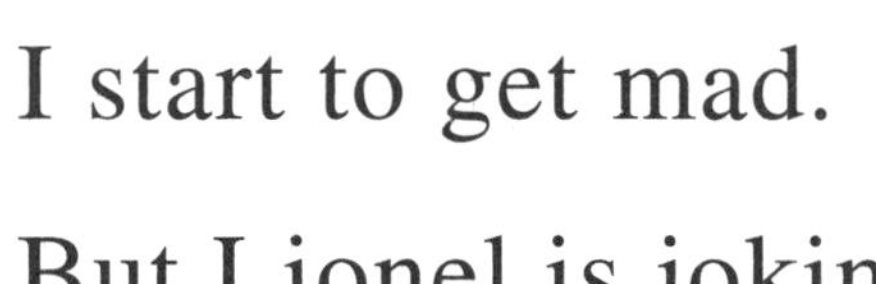

I start to get mad.
But Lionel is joking again.
He really means that he's glad
we're on the same team.
It's Backward Day!

Later Ms. Glass says,

“What shall we do next?

I have no more backward ideas.”

I look around the room
at all the topsy-turvy outfits.
Ooh la la! I have an idea.
"Let's have a fashion show—
a backward fashion show."

Lionel makes a face.

So do some other boys.

"No!" he says.

"Fashion shows are no fun."

This time Lionel is not joking.

“Ha-ha!” I shout.
“This time YOU forgot.
It’s Backward Day.
You just said that
fashion shows ARE fun.”

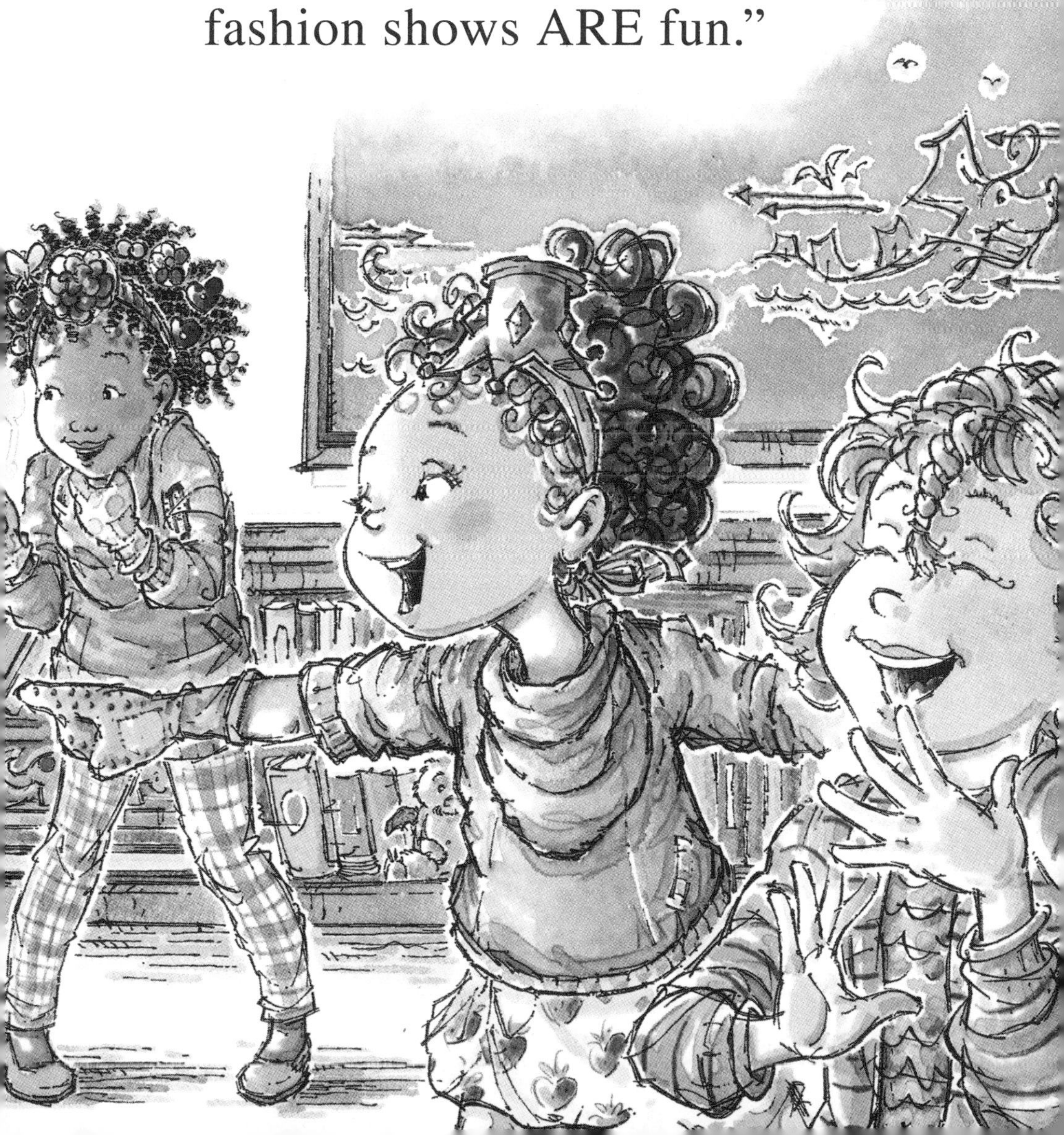

Lionel knows I got him this time.

We all model our ensembles.

Ensemble is fancy for clothes.

54321

After the fashion show,
it’s time to go home.
“Hello,” we say to Ms. Glass.
“See you yesterday.”

And that is the beginning—
I mean the end—
of this story.

Fancy Nancy's Fancy Words

These are the fancy words in this book:

Delectable—yummy

Ensemble—clothes

Extremely—very

Nonsensical—super silly

Topsy-turvy—upside down and super silly